Where's Harley?

by Carol and Amanda Felton
Illustrated by Page Eastburn O'Rourke

The Kane Press
New York

Book Design/Art Direction: Roberta Pressel

Library of Congress Cataloging-in-Publication Data

Felton, Carol.
    Where's Harley?/by Carol and Amanda Felton; illustrated by Page Eastburn O'Rourke.—[1st U.S. ed.].
      p. cm. — (Math matters.)
    Summary: Two children search their apartment building from the first floor to the tenth, but their pet rabbit stays one hop ahead of them.
    ISBN 1-57565-132-7 (alk. paper)
    [1. Rabbits—Fiction. 2. Lost and found possessions—Fiction. 3. Numbers, Ordinal—Fiction.] I. Felton, Amanda. II. O'Rourke, Page Eastburn, ill. III. Title. IV. Series.
    PZ7.F33687 Wh 2003
    [E]—dc21
    2002156248

10 9 8 7 6 5 4 3

First published in the United States of America in 2003 by The Kane Press.
Printed in Hong Kong.

MATH MATTERS® is a registered trademark of The Kane Press.

Mandy and Nate live on the sixth floor.
The first thing they do after school is take
care of Harley. Harley is their pet rabbit.

"You feed him and I'll cuddle him," says Nate.

"Oh, thanks," says Mandy. "I work while you play!" She goes into the kitchen and gets the carrots.

Carrots are Harley's favorite food.

"We're home, Harley." Nate calls. He
goes out to the terrace.

But Harley is not in his hutch.

"Oh, no!" Nate yells. "Where is Harley?"

Mandy and Nate look everywhere—
under the beds, behind the chairs,
inside the closets.
But no Harley.

They even look out in the hall.

Nate looks behind a box of flowers. "No Harley," he says.

Mandy looks inside the umbrella stand. "He's not in here, either," she says.

Mandy calls their friends.
Maria lives on the eighth floor.
Gus lives on the fourth floor.
"Meet us at our apartment. Harley escaped!"
Mandy tells them. "Bring your walkie-talkies."

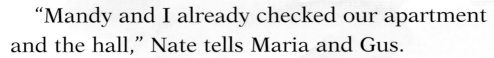

"Mandy and I already checked our apartment and the hall," Nate tells Maria and Gus.

"We'd better check all the floors," says Maria.

"Nate, you and Maria look upstairs," says Mandy. "Gus and I will go downstairs."

Mandy reports from the fifth floor.
"Harley was here!" she says. "The pizza
guy says he saw a rabbit!"
But where is Harley now?

Harley is munching on leaves.

Gus and Mandy walk down to the
fourth floor.

"Harley was here!" Gus says. "I see
his tooth marks on my mom's plant!"

But where is Harley now?

Harley is cleaning his fur.

Mandy reports from the third floor.

"Harley was here!" she says. "I found some rabbit hairs!"

But where is Harley now?

Harley is making a friend.

Gus and Mandy go down to the second floor. "Harley was here!" Gus says. "Baby Sarah is saying, 'Bunny! Bunny!'"

But where is Harley now?

Harley is going for a ride.

Maria and Nate report from the tenth floor.
"Harley was here!" Nate says. "I see his footprints on the wet floor!"
But where is Harley now?

Harley is getting a scare!

| 10th |
| 9th |
| 8th |
| 7th |
| 6th |
| 5th |
| 4th |
| 3rd |
| 2nd |
| 1st |

Maria reports from the ninth floor.
"Harley was here!" she says. "Can you
hear me? Rex won't stop barking!"
But where is Harley now?

Harley is trying to hide.

Nate and Maria hurry to the eighth floor.
"Harley was here!" Nate says. "I found a
towel, and it smells like Harley!"
But where is Harley now?

Harley is taking a nap.

Maria reports from the seventh floor.
"No sign of Harley here!" she says.
"We don't know where else to look,"
says Nate.

"Let's all meet
on the first floor,"
says Mandy.

Nate and Maria ride down to the first floor.

"We found lots of clues," says Gus.

"But no Harley," Nate says.

"He just keeps one hop ahead of us," says Maria.

"We can't give up," Mandy says.

"That's my towel!" says Mrs. Lundy.
"Thanks!" She puts it in the laundry cart.
Nate spots something in Mrs. Lundy's
cart. It's white. It's round. It's fluffy.
"It's Harley's tail!" Nate yells.

Nate reaches into the laundry cart and
pulls out—Mrs. Lundy's sweater!
Oops!

"We're never going to find him," says Nate.
"I'm tired," says Maria.
"Me, too," says Gus.
"I'm hungry," says Nate.
"Here, have a carrot!" says Mandy.

Something warm and furry hops from behind some boxes.

"Harley! We found you!" Nate shouts. He gives Harley a big hug.

Mandy laughs. "I think Harley found us—"

"AND the carrots!" says Nate.

Where is Harley now?

With his best friends!

ORDINAL NUMBERS CHART

Some special numbers tell you about ORDER.

I know! Numbers like FIRST, SECOND, and THIRD!

One type of ORDER: from bottom to top

10th	tenth floor
9th	ninth floor
8th	eighth floor ➡ Maria lives here.
7th	seventh floor
6th	sixth floor ➡ Nate and Mandy live here.
5th	fifth floor
4th	fourth floor ➡ Gus lives here.
3rd	third floor
2nd	second floor
1st	first floor

Another type of ORDER: from left to right in a line

first   second   third   fourth   fifth   sixth   seventh   eighth   ninth   tenth